A Lost Soul

By Maryam Husain

Rediscovering What Truly Matters

Published by Mahu Creation

Disclaimer

This is a work of fiction. Names, characters, organizations, places, events, and incidents are either products of the author's imagination or are used fictitiously. Any resemblance to actual persons, living or dead, or actual events is purely coincidental.

Published by Mahu Creation First Edition, January 2025

For inquiries or more information, visit Instagram - **@iammahu_**
@explore_with_mahu

Introduction

In the fast-paced world we live in today, it's easy to get lost in the noise. The quest for approval, external validation, and societal expectations often distract us from our true selves. A Lost Soul follows the journey of Amira, a teenager who falls into the trap of seeking worldly pleasures and chasing perfection on social media. From the outside, her life appears flawless – she's popular, has a large following, and is surrounded by friends. But inside, she feels empty, disconnected, and unsure of what truly matters.

Throughout this book, you will walk with Amira as she battles her internal demons, confronts the consequences of her distractions, and slowly begins the painful yet rewarding process of self-discovery. Her story is filled with struggles, tough decisions, and moments of clarity. But ultimately, it is about finding one's way back to what is truly important – love, self-acceptance, and the realisation that happiness comes from within, not from the approval of others.

This book is not just a story; it's a reflection of our own lives. A reminder that we all have the power to change, to refocus, and to reconnect with who we really are. A Lost Soul is an invitation to reflect, learn, and perhaps find the courage to reclaim your life from the distractions that surround us.

Table of Contents

This story serves as a gentle reminder for all of us: no matter how lost we feel, there's always a way back to our true selves.

So, turn the page, dive in, and embark on a journey of self-discovery with Amira.

Chapter 1:
The Perfect Illusion

Amira sat on her bed, eyes glued to the screen of her phone, as the soft glow illuminated her face. The room around her was quiet, yet inside her, a storm of thoughts raged. She had uploaded another picture—a selfie, perfectly taken in the best light, from the best angle, with just enough editing to make it look flawless. The comments started rolling in almost immediately. "You look stunning," "Gorgeous as always," "Queen of the gram." Each like, each comment, each new follower felt like an instant rush, a fleeting high she couldn't get enough of.

It wasn't just about the image; it was about validation. The more people liked her, the more she felt seen, valued, important. It became an addiction.
She couldn't go a few minutes without checking her notifications, almost as if her self-worth was tied to how many people appreciated her online presence. It was like an invisible drug, and she was hooked.

She scrolled through her feed, stopping to like a few photos, comment here and there. Her friends were doing the same. The group chats buzzed with discussions about the latest trends, outfits, and updates. They were all part of this new world, a world that revolved around appearances, followers, and approval. Amira liked it. She loved the attention, the compliments, the sense of importance that came with being popular on social media.

But deep down, something unsettled her. The high from the likes faded quickly, leaving behind a nagging emptiness. Was this all there was to life? Was she chasing a dream that was never really hers to begin with? She dismissed the thought, shoving it aside. After all, everyone was doing it. Everyone was trying to build an image, a persona, an online world
that was more "perfect" than the real one. Was it really so wrong to want to fit in, to be admired?

"Amira, hurry up, we're going to be late!" Maya's voice broke through her thoughts.

Amira quickly glanced at the time. She had a few minutes left before school started. She tossed her phone onto the bed and grabbed her bag, making sure to pack her makeup kit and phone charger. She couldn't forget her essentials. As she left her room, her mind lingered on the phone screen, still buzzing with new notifications.

At school, Amira's routine was the same. Between classes, during lunch breaks, and even while walking through the halls, she checked her social media. It had become second nature. Every moment, every exchange was an opportunity to capture the perfect shot, to document every part of her life and present it to the world in the best possible way.

But as she sat in class, listening to the teacher, a small voice whispered in her mind again. What was the point of all this? What was she really gaining from all the likes and comments? She knew deep down that these fleeting moments of validation weren't enough to fill the growing emptiness inside her. But she couldn't stop. It was a cycle—one she wasn't sure how to break.

By the end of the day, Amira was exhausted. She had gained followers, received hundreds of likes, but the emptiness remained. The perfect illusion she had created was beginning to crumble, but she wasn't ready to face it yet.

She opened her phone once more, hoping for the rush of new notifications to fill the void. But this time, it didn't feel the same…….. To be continued…..

Chapter 2: The Fading Light

Amira stood in front of the mirror, adjusting her hair for the umpteenth time that morning. She couldn't shake off the feeling that something was off. The reflection staring back at her was the same—flawless makeup, perfectly styled hair, the latest fashion—but it felt empty. The glowing screen of her phone sat on the vanity beside her, filled with notifications. Messages from friends, comments from strangers, all offering praise and validation. But somehow, it wasn't enough anymore.

Her followers had grown over the past few months, and so had her social media presence. The attention was intoxicating, but the thrill was beginning to wear off. There was a hollowness in her chest that she couldn't ignore. Every like, every comment felt increasingly insignificant, as if it couldn't fill the gap that was growing inside her. What was she really chasing?

She grabbed her phone, scrolling through the endless feed. New outfits, vacation photos, selfies—everyone seemed to be living their best lives. But instead of feeling connected, she felt more alone than ever. The digital world she had once poured her heart into now felt like a hollow shell. She compared herself to everyone, always feeling like she was falling short,

like she wasn't measuring up to the perfect lives others seemed to lead.

At school, the distractions continued. She had once been at the center of every conversation, every group chat, but now, it felt different. Her friends seemed to be focused on their own lives—posts, updates, and drama—and less on the meaningful connections that used to matter. Maya had noticed, too.

"Amira, are you okay?" Maya asked one afternoon, as they sat on the bleachers during lunch. "You've been kind of distant lately. You barely talk anymore."

Amira forced a smile, brushing off the concern. "I'm fine. Just a little tired, that's all."

But deep down, Amira knew she wasn't fine. Her grades were slipping, something she hadn't cared about before. Her focus was on maintaining her online persona, not her future. Her social media presence had become her identity—her worth measured in followers, likes, and comments. Yet, the more she sought external validation, the more she felt lost within herself.

The realization hit her in class one day, during a test she had barely studied for. The questions on the page seemed foreign to her, as if she had been living in a different reality. Her thoughts kept drifting back to her phone, to the constant craving for attention. Her grades had fallen drastically, but she didn't know how to fix it. She had sacrificed so much of her real life to maintain the illusion of perfection online.

She failed the test. It wasn't the first time, but this time, the weight of it felt different. It felt like the tipping point.

That evening, she sat on her bed, staring at the screen. The comments kept pouring in, but the validation felt increasingly hollow. Was this the life she wanted? To be stuck in a cycle of empty likes and superficial connections? She had no answers.
But the questions kept gnawing at her.

The following day, something inside her shifted. She deleted a few of her apps, then stared at the empty spaces on her phone. It was freeing in a way, but also terrifying. How would she fill the silence now? She didn't know who she was without the validation of her followers, but she was about to find out.

Amira was beginning to realize that the light she had once followed—the constant stream of likes, the attention, the false connection—was fading. And in its place, a deeper question emerged: What would she find if she stepped away from it all? What would she discover about herself in the quiet moments?

Chapter 3:
The Price of Popularity

Amira sat at her desk, the soft glow of her phone illuminating her face. She had been staring at the screen for what felt like hours, her thumb scrolling through endless notifications, each one a reminder of her success—or so she thought. The likes, the comments, the followers—it was all supposed to make her feel validated, important, special. But now, in the quiet of her room, they felt hollow, empty. The rush of dopamine that used to flood her every time she posted a picture or received a compliment had started to wane. It wasn't enough anymore.

Her mind raced as she reflected on the price she had paid for this life of constant attention and approval. The last few months had been a whirlwind of photoshoots, events, and parties—all for the sake of maintaining her social media presence. But with every post, every update, every new follower, she had lost a little more of herself. The carefully curated life she projected online wasn't real. It was a mask, a facade she had built to hide the emptiness she felt inside.

Her phone buzzed again, breaking her thoughts. She glanced at the notification—a message from Maya, her best friend: "Hey, are you coming over later? I miss you."

Amira paused for a moment, feeling a pang of guilt.

She hadn't spent real time with Maya in weeks. Their friendship had been strained, not because of any major fallout, but because Amira had been so consumed by her online life that she barely had time for anything else. Maya had always been there for her, but Amira had pushed her away without even realizing it.

She typed a quick reply, trying to sound casual.

"Sure, I'll be there in a bit. Just finishing some stuff up."

The truth was, she wasn't really "finishing stuff up." She was scrolling through her Instagram feed, comparing herself to everyone else. The endless cycle of checking her likes, reading the comments, and scrolling through everyone else's perfect lives had become an addiction. She couldn't stop, even though part of her knew it was doing more harm than good.

When she arrived at Maya's house, the first thing she noticed was the way her best friend looked at her.
Maya's eyes were filled with concern, but she didn't say anything immediately. Instead, she led Amira into the living room, where they sat down together.

"So, what's going on, Amira?" Maya asked, her voice gentle. "You've been acting weird lately. You're always on your phone, always posting, but you seem… distant."

Amira felt a wave of defensiveness rise up in her.

She didn't want to admit that she was struggling, that the life she had built was starting to crumble. But Maya had always been able to see through her, and today was no exception.

"I don't know, Maya," Amira replied, staring down at her hands. "I thought I had it all figured out. I thought being popular, having a lot of followers, and being seen by everyone would make me happy. But it doesn't. It's like I'm trapped in this world that I can't escape from. And the more I try to keep up, the more I feel like I'm losing myself."

Maya didn't say anything at first. She just sat there, listening, her eyes full of empathy. Finally, she spoke.

"Amira, popularity isn't everything. You don't have to keep chasing after validation from people who
don't really know you. The people who care about you are the ones who will be there, no matter what.

You're more than your followers, more than your posts. Don't let this fake world dictate your worth."

Amira's heart ached as she listened to Maya's words. She had heard them before, but this time, they hit differently. Deep down, she knew Maya was right. The popularity she had worked so hard to achieve came at a cost—a cost that was too high. She had lost sight of who she was, of the things that truly mattered. And now, the pressure of maintaining her online persona was weighing on her, making her feel like she was constantly performing, constantly trying to be someone she wasn't.

For the first time in months, Amira felt a sense of relief. It was as if a weight had been lifted off her shoulders. She didn't have to keep pretending. She didn't have to keep living for the approval of others.

That night, as Amira lay in bed, she thought about everything that had brought her to this point. She had spent so much time chasing after likes and followers, thinking that those things would fill the emptiness inside her. But they hadn't. The void remained, and the more she sought validation from others, the more distant she had become from herself.

She closed her eyes, taking a deep breath, and made a decision. She was done with the endless cycle of comparison and validation. It was time to take control of her life, to stop living for the approval of others, and to start living for herself. She didn't need to be famous or popular to be happy. What she needed was peace, self-acceptance, and real connections with the people who mattered most.

As she drifted off to sleep that night, a new sense of determination filled her. She didn't know exactly what the future held, but she knew one thing for sure: she wasn't going to let the price of popularity control her life any longer.

Chapter 4:
A World of Distractions

Amira sat at her desk, the pile of textbooks in front of her seeming more like an insurmountable mountain than a source of knowledge. The pages were filled with information—dates, facts, equations—but they all blurred together. She tried to focus, tried to concentrate on the task at hand, but it was impossible. Her phone was sitting right beside her, like a silent temptress, begging for attention. Every few minutes, she would pick it up, swipe through her notifications, and scroll mindlessly through the endless stream of posts.

It had become a habit. A reflex.

Her studies had been pushed aside, her homework left unfinished, and her grades were slipping. She knew it, but she couldn't stop. The urge to stay connected, to be in the loop, was overwhelming.

Every ping, every notification felt like a jolt of electricity running through her. It was as if her phone had become an extension of her body, a constant companion that she couldn't put down.

She glanced at the clock. It was almost midnight, and the pages of her history textbook remained as untouched as when she had first opened it. She had been sitting here for hours, scrolling through her feed, looking at other people's lives—lives that seemed so much more exciting, more fulfilling than her own. There was one post after another: vacation photos, new clothes, parties, selfies—all of it serving as a reminder of what she didn't have. It was as if the world was going on without her, and she was stuck in an endless loop of comparison and regret.

Amira had become trapped in a world of distractions.

It wasn't just her phone, though. Everywhere she went, there were distractions. At school, the classrooms were filled with people texting under the desk, checking Instagram and Snapchat in between lessons. At lunch, the cafeteria was a sea of heads buried in screens, the sounds of conversations replaced by the clicking of buttons. Even at home, it seemed like there was no escape. The television was on, her parents were busy with their own devices, and her mind wandered back to the glow of her phone.

The noise was constant, the distractions unrelenting. She would wake up in the morning, and the first thing she did was check her phone.

She would scroll through her social media apps, checking for any updates, any new likes, any new followers. It had become a ritual—a ritual that started her day, but also drained her of any sense of purpose.

She couldn't remember the last time she woke up without the urge to check her notifications. It was as if her entire sense of self had become wrapped up in how others saw her, how many people cared enough to engage with her posts.

But as time went on, Amira started to feel the weight of it all. She felt disconnected from herself, lost in a sea of digital noise. Every like, every comment, every new post felt like it was never enough. There was always something more, something better. If she posted a picture and didn't get enough likes, she would feel a pang of disappointment, a sinking feeling that maybe she wasn't good enough. Maybe she wasn't as beautiful, as interesting, as worth following as others. And so, the cycle continued.

One afternoon, after another long day at school,
Amira sat alone in her room, staring at her phone. She had just posted a new picture—a selfie she had taken while getting ready for school. The caption was clever, the filters perfect. But as she waited for the likes to roll in, she couldn't shake the feeling that it wasn't enough. She felt empty, like there was something missing in her life that no number of likes or comments could ever fill.

She realized, for the first time, that she had been so caught up in the virtual world, she had forgotten to live in the real one. The distractions had taken over every aspect of her life. The pursuit of likes, validation, and popularity had become her sole focus. It was as if she had built a wall around herself, a wall made of digital approval, and now she was trapped behind it.

Her mind wandered to the past, to a time when things had been different. When she hadn't felt the constant need to check her phone, to make sure she was staying on top of the trends, to make sure her life was as perfect as everyone else's. It seemed so long ago, a different version of herself. She used to enjoy the simple things— reading a book, spending time with her family, laughing with friends without worrying about getting the perfect selfie. But now, those things felt distant, like relics from another time.

Her thoughts were interrupted by a knock on the door. It was Maya. Amira had been so absorbed in her phone that she hadn't even heard her friend arrive.

"Hey, are you okay?" Maya asked, stepping into the room. "I haven't seen you in a while, and you're always on your phone."

Amira looked up, a mix of guilt and frustration rising inside her. "I don't know, Maya. I'm just… I feel like I'm losing myself. All I do is check my phone, check my likes, see what everyone else is doing, and I'm just… tired. Tired of pretending that this is all that matters."

Maya walked over and sat down next to her. "You don't have to keep up with everyone else, Amira.
You're enough as you are. Social media isn't real.
It's just a highlight reel of people's lives, and everyone is comparing themselves to everyone else.

But at the end of the day, it's all just a distraction from what really matters."

Amira took a deep breath, her friend's words sinking in. For the first time in weeks, she felt a sense of clarity. She had been so consumed by distractions that she had forgotten to live for herself. The constant stream of notifications, the likes, the comments, they were never going to bring her the happiness she was searching for.

Maybe it was time to step away, to unplug, and to start living in the moment again.

Chapter 5:
The Breaking Point

The days had blurred together in a haze of social media posts, fake smiles, and an overwhelming feeling of emptiness. Amira had continued to scroll through her phone, constantly looking for the next like, the next comment, the next affirmation. Yet, no matter how much she received, it never felt like enough. Each day seemed to drain her more, leaving her feeling hollow and disconnected. It was as if she were standing on the edge of a cliff, staring into a chasm of uncertainty, with no way to turn back.

Her grades had plummeted. Her friends had begun to notice her absence, but she didn't seem to care. Every moment was consumed by the need to be perfect, to be admired, to be seen. She had become

so accustomed to the constant flow of attention online that she couldn't understand why it no longer satisfied her. The illusion of happiness that social media had promised felt fragile, like a house of cards teetering on the verge of collapse.

It was a Friday afternoon when the tipping point came. Amira had just posted a new picture, one that she had spent hours perfecting. The lighting had to be just right. The angle had to highlight her best features. She had picked the perfect outfit, and every detail was curated for maximum engagement. It was, by all accounts, a flawless post.

But when she checked her phone after a few minutes, she was hit with a wave of frustration. The likes were trickling in at a slower pace than usual. The comments were fewer, the engagement lackluster.

Amira's heart sank as she saw the number of likes barely surpassing the 100 mark. She had been used to hundreds, even thousands of likes within the first few minutes of posting. This, this felt different. This was a failure.

Her mind raced with questions. Why isn't anyone liking it? Did I post at the wrong time? Is something wrong with my caption? Am I not pretty enough? Not interesting enough? The familiar anxiety that had plagued her for weeks bubbled to the surface. She refreshed the screen over and over, hoping for more likes, for validation that never came.

She sat there, frozen, her fingers hovering over the screen, desperately waiting for the numbers to climb. But they didn't.

It was in that moment, when the last few remnants of her self-worth seemed to unravel, that Amira finally saw the truth. The bright, colorful world of social media that she had clung to for so long was nothing but a mirage—a carefully constructed illusion designed to trap her in a cycle of never-ending comparison. Every time she had thought she had achieved something, it was always followed by a deeper sense of emptiness. It was as if the more she chased after perfection, the further it slipped out of her grasp.

She put her phone down with a trembling hand, the weight of it heavy in her lap. The room felt smaller, suffocating even, as the realization washed over her.

This isn't who I am. This isn't what I want. The thought was terrifying, but it also felt liberating in a way she couldn't explain.

For years, Amira had been chasing validation, living for the approval of others, only to discover that it would never fill the hole she felt inside. Her phone, once a source of joy and excitement, had now become a symbol of her disconnection from the real world. She had traded meaningful experiences, authentic relationships, and her own happiness for the fleeting gratification of likes and comments.

But the breaking point didn't just come from the frustration of a low-engagement post. It was the culmination of everything that had been building up in her life—the late nights spent scrolling through her feed instead of studying, the missed moments with friends because she was busy curating her online image, the hollow feeling that seemed to linger long after she put her phone down. It was the constant pressure to keep up with everyone else, to keep posting, to keep sharing, to keep up the facade of a perfect life.

The next few hours were a blur. Amira's mind raced with questions and doubts. She was angry, sad, confused—all at once. She had built her identity around her online persona, but now she was beginning to wonder who she really was beneath all of that. What had she become? Was this really the life she wanted? Was the constant pursuit of perfection worth it?

Later that evening, she received a text from Maya:

"Are you okay? I haven't heard from you all day."

Amira stared at the message for a long time before responding. She felt the weight of the words she had to say next, knowing that this conversation could change everything.

"I don't know, Maya. I think I'm lost. I don't know who I am anymore."

Maya responded almost immediately: "You're not lost, Amira. You just have to find yourself again.
You don't need to be perfect. You don't need to keep up with everyone else. You just need to be you."

For the first time in a long time, Amira felt a sense of calm. Maya's words resonated with her, and for the first time, she allowed herself to breathe. She had been running from herself, trying to fit into a mold that wasn't hers. The pressure to be perfect, to be admired, had pushed her further away from her true self.

She stood up, walking over to her window and looking out at the city lights below. For a moment, the noise of the world around her seemed to fade. It was as if she could hear her own thoughts, her own voice, for the first time in ages. The urge to check her phone was still there, but it no longer felt as urgent. It no longer felt as important.

In that quiet moment, Amira made a decision. She would stop chasing the approval of others. She would stop living for the likes and comments. She would stop allowing her worth to be determined by the number of followers she had or the number of hearts on her posts. It wouldn't be easy. It wouldn't happen overnight. But Amira knew that in order to find herself, she had to let go of the distractions. She had to stop pretending, stop performing, and start living authentically.

With a deep breath, she powered off her phone, setting it down on her desk. For the first time in years, she felt free.

Chapter 6: Falling Apart

Amira couldn't escape it. The nagging feeling that something was terribly wrong with her life had been growing for weeks now, gnawing at her from the inside. Each day felt like a battle, a war between the mask she had carefully crafted for the world and the shattered person she had become from inside. She had tried to shake it off—tried to numb the emptiness with more likes, more followers, more perfect selfies—but the emptiness only deepened. No matter how many posts she uploaded, no matter how many notifications buzzed in her pocket, it was never enough.

The truth was that Amira didn't feel like herself anymore. The version of her that existed online—the flawless, picture-perfect girl who lived for the camera—had taken over the real Amira, the one who used to laugh with friends without worrying about her appearance or spend hours daydreaming instead of calculating how many likes her next post would get.

But now, those moments felt like a distant memory. Her mind was constantly preoccupied with numbers—how many likes, how many comments, how many new followers. She had traded her selfworth for a screen, and no matter how much she achieved online, it was never enough. Every time she checked her notifications, the numbers never seemed to bring the satisfaction they once did. The small victories that once gave her a fleeting sense of accomplishment had long since lost their power. It was as if a part of her had died, and no amount of validation could bring her back to life.

The feeling of falling apart was becoming unbearable. She had always prided herself on her ability to manage everything—school, friends, social media. She was the girl who seemed to have it all together. But now, the facade was beginning to crumble. Her grades had taken a nosedive. She had stopped caring about homework, stopped caring about studying. It felt irrelevant compared to the allconsuming need to keep up the appearance of the perfect life. It wasn't just the grades, either. Her friendships were starting to unravel. Maya, once her closest friend, had grown distant. Amira had ignored her calls, too wrapped up in her own spiral to notice the signs of concern.

It had been two days since Maya had sent her the text that had started to shake Amira's perception of everything: "You don't seem like yourself lately.
Please talk to me. I'm worried about you."

Amira had read the message over and over, her heart sinking each time. She didn't know how to respond.

She wasn't ready to admit that everything she had worked so hard for—her online persona, her perfect life—was falling apart. She didn't know how to explain that the world she had built around herself felt like a prison now, suffocating her with its expectations.

Her phone buzzed again, pulling her out of her thoughts. Another notification. Another comment. But this time, the rush of dopamine she had once felt was replaced with a wave of disgust. She looked at her phone in disgust, her eyes scanning the comments that flooded in like an avalanche. "You're such an inspiration," one read. "I wish I had your life," said another.

But all she could feel was a cold emptiness. None of this was real. She wasn't real. The likes didn't mean anything. The comments were empty. It was all just noise, distractions from the real issues that were slowly tearing her apart.

She had always been praised for her beauty, her charm, her seemingly perfect life. But what happened when that mask started to crack? What happened when the world you had created around yourself felt more like a cage than a refuge? Amira didn't know the answer, but she knew she couldn't keep pretending. She couldn't keep living a life that wasn't hers.

The more she thought about it, the more overwhelmed she became. She had spent so many years chasing this illusion of perfection, and now, standing on the other side of it, she saw it for what it really was—empty, shallow, meaningless. The more followers she gained, the more she lost herself. And the emptier she felt, the more she wanted to disappear from it all.

She pulled her legs up to her chest and wrapped her arms around her knees, sitting on the floor of her bedroom. The walls seemed to close in around her, suffocating her. The pressure was too much. She felt like she was suffocating. She closed her eyes tightly, trying to block out the noise—the constant stream of notifications, the endless comparisons to others, the relentless drive to keep up appearances. But it was all too much. It felt like the weight of the world was pressing down on her, and she couldn't breathe.

Amira had always prided herself on being in control, on being the girl who had it all figured out. But now, she felt like she was spiraling out of control, like a leaf caught in the wind, helpless to stop the chaos that was unfolding in her life.

The tears came before she even realized it. She felt them sliding down her face, hot and unfamiliar, and it felt like the floodgates had opened. She had spent so much time holding everything in, pretending that she was fine when she was far from it. But now, the weight of it all was too much to bear.

She picked up her phone again, staring at it as if it held all the answers. The bright screen seemed almost mocking in its silence. She had become addicted to the need for validation, and now that it wasn't fulfilling her anymore, she was left with nothing. It was a cruel irony—her phone, the source of her pain and her addiction, was also the tool that had given her a sense of purpose for so long.

Amira took a deep breath, her hands trembling as she stared at the screen. She couldn't keep doing this.

She couldn't keep chasing something that wasn't real, something that would never make her feel whole. She needed to let go of the illusion. She needed to find her way back to herself.

It wasn't an easy decision. It wasn't something she could do in a single moment. But at that moment, with tears in her eyes and a heaviness in her chest, Amira made a promise to herself. She was done pretending. She was done chasing an image of perfection that wasn't hers to begin with.

She powered off her phone, the soft hummm of the device dying in her hand. For the first time in weeks, she didn't feel the urge to pick it up again. It wasn't the answer to her problems. It wasn't the key to her happiness. And for once, she felt a small glimmer of hope.

Amira didn't know what the future held, but she knew one thing for sure: she couldn't keep living like this. She couldn't keep drowning in a world of distractions and illusions. She had to find herself again, even if it meant walking away from everything she had built.

Chapter 7:
The Wake-Up Call

Amira woke up to the harsh glare of sunlight piercing through the curtains, casting long shadows across the room. Her head throbbed. The weight of the previous night's exhaustion lingered in her body, and her mind felt like it was wrapped in fog. She stared at the ceiling for a moment, trying to make sense of the feeling that had gnawed at her for weeks, but never with such intensity as it did now. It wasn't a hangover from alcohol—she hadn't touched a drop in months. It wasn't physical exhaustion from schoolwork or extra curriculars. This was something else. Something deeper. Something harder to shake.

The world outside her window seemed far away, untouched by the turmoil that seemed to swirl inside her. She sighed and reached for her phone, the automatic motion almost as reflexive as breathing. She had promised herself just yesterday that she wouldn't check it first thing in the morning—that she would try to get a grip on her life before allowing the endless cycle of notifications and digital validation to suck her back in. But as soon as her hand grazed the cold glass of her phone, she felt a wave of compulsion wash over her. What if there was something important? What if Maya had texted her again? Or maybe there was a new comment that would make her feel better?

But as her thumb hovered over the screen, Amira hesitated. For the first time, she realized just how little control she had over this behavior. The pull of her phone had become an addiction, and it wasn't just harmless scrolling. It was a need—a desperate one. She couldn't go an hour, sometimes even a minute, without checking it.

But today, something in her snapped. She wasn't sure why, but in that moment, she knew that she had to stop. She had to break free from the cycle, or it would consume her completely. She set the phone back down on the nightstand, the cold plastic almost as if rejecting her. It wasn't the phone's fault, she knew, but rather the attachment she had allowed herself to develop to it. Her entire sense of self had become wrapped up in that small, glowing screen, and she didn't want to be that person anymore.

A long while, Amira decided to do something different. She dragged herself out of bed, her legs stiff and her body sluggish, but there was a fire igniting inside her—something she hadn't felt in months. She was determined to find herself again. To live outside the screen and reclaim the girl she had once been, before likes, followers, and digital validation had controlled her every move.

The first step was to get out of the house. Her mother had been worried about her for weeks now, but
Amira hadn't given her the time of day. She had become so consumed with her own problems that she couldn't see the ones affecting her family. She could feel the weight of her mother's concerned eyes

every time they spoke, but Amira had been too self absorbed to acknowledge it.

As Amira stepped out into the crisp morning air, she felt a slight pang of guilt for having ignored her family. Her mother's gentle reminders, her little notes on the kitchen table about eating healthy, her presence in the background, always there, always worried. Amira had taken it for granted, choosing to be distracted by the noise of the online world instead. But now, the realization hit her hard—what had she been running from? Her mother wasn't the problem. The problem was her addiction to an image, a facade, a screen.

She grabbed her jacket and stepped outside, the cool morning air biting at her skin. The world was quieter here, without the constant noise of social media. The simple act of breathing in fresh air, of being alive in the present moment, felt foreign but strangely comforting. Amira walked, her feet carrying her down the familiar path to the park, the place where she used to come to think—before everything had changed.

She hadn't been here in months. The benches in the park were empty, the trees swaying gently in the breeze. It felt like a world apart from the chaos she had created for herself. Her feet dragged on the path, and she felt the weight of her choices pressing down on her. Was it too late? Could she fix what she had done? Could she reclaim the life she had abandoned for the sake of appearances?

As she sat down on one of the benches, she closed her eyes and let the peace of the moment wash over her. It was strange how still the world seemed compared to the constant buzz of her phone. She realized just how disconnected she had become from everything that mattered. All the time she had spent on her phone, scrolling through other people's lives, had caused her to lose touch with her own. She had forgotten what it felt like to sit and think without needing constant validation from others.

But then, like a hammer hitting her consciousness, a thought struck her: How had she gotten here?

Amira had once been so full of life, so curious about the world, so connected to the people around her. She had made friends, had real conversations, spent time doing things that brought her joy—like reading, painting, running through the streets at sunset with Maya. But somewhere along the way, all of that had faded.

The need for digital validation had crept in slowly, like a poison. She had started with just a few photos—selfies with filters, cute captions—but those likes, those comments, had fed her ego. They made her feel important. They made her feel wanted. And slowly, the drive for external approval had overtaken her sense of self. She had replaced real relationships with the dopamine hit of new followers. She had traded her happiness for fleeting moments of attention from strangers who would never truly know her.

But now, sitting in the quiet of the park, Amira realized just how hollow it all felt. All of the attention, all of the likes, all of the followers—none of it was real. It was a carefully curated illusion that she had spent so much time trying to perfect, but it had never truly filled the emptiness she had been carrying around.

As she sat there, a sense of clarity began to form. Maybe this was the wake-up call she needed. Maybe this was the moment when everything would change.
She didn't want to continue down this path. She didn't want to live for the approval of strangers. She wanted to live for herself—for the real, unfiltered version of herself.

But she knew it wouldn't be easy. Letting go of social media meant disconnecting from the very thing that had defined her for so long. It meant shedding the image she had so carefully constructed. It meant facing the fear of being unknown, of being ordinary. And yet, as she stared at the blue sky above her, she felt a flicker of hope.

She had spent so much time trying to fit into a world that wasn't hers. A world where likes and followers determined self-worth. A world where superficiality had replaced depth. But now, for the first time, she realized that there was more to life than the perfect selfie, more than the number of hearts next to her post. There was peace in being herself, in being present in her own life.

And so, with a deep breath, Amira made a decision. She was going to step back from social media, at least for a while. She was going to reconnect with the things she loved, the things that had once brought her peace. She was going to reclaim her life from the digital world that had consumed it.

It wasn't going to be easy, and she knew there would be moments of doubt. But in a long time, Amira felt hopeful. She had taken the first step towards finding herself again. The road ahead might be difficult, but at least now, she was ready to walk it. She could only hope that it would lead her back to the girl she had once been.

As she left the park and returned home, her heart felt lighter. There was still a long way to go, but for the first time in ages, she felt like she was moving in the right direction.

Chapter 8: Seeking Answers

The days following Amira's decision to delete her social media apps felt like stepping into a fog. Each moment was clouded with uncertainty, and she couldn't quite shake the feeling that something was missing. It was strange, this quiet existence. Without the constant buzz of notifications and the need to check her phone every few minutes, there was an unsettling void she couldn't quite fill. It was like a piece of her had been ripped away, leaving her grasping for something she couldn't name.

She spent the first few days in silence, lost in her thoughts, reflecting on everything that had led her to this point. The need for validation, the pursuit of perfection—it all seemed so hollow now. But the question that haunted her the most was why she had ever allowed herself to fall into that trap in the first place.

The real answers, the ones that could help her make sense of everything, seemed just out of reach, like a distant memory she couldn't quite remember. Why had she needed to be seen by so many people? Why had she felt like her worth was determined by the number of likes on her posts?

To answer these questions, Amira knew she had to look deeper than the surface level. She needed to confront her insecurities, her fears, and the parts of herself she had spent so long hiding.

One evening, as she sat on the balcony, her mind wandered back to a conversation she had had with her mother a few days earlier. It was a quiet moment in the kitchen, just the two of them, when her mother had asked her, "Amira, what do you really want? What makes you happy?"

At the time, Amira had brushed it off with a quick answer. "I don't know, Mom. I'm fine." But now, sitting in the stillness of the evening, she realized that her answer had been a lie. She wasn't fine. She wasn't okay with just living for validation, for the next post or comment. She wanted more. She wanted to be seen—not for the filters, the perfect pictures, or the idealized version of herself that she had shared with the world—but for who she really was.

It was a terrifying thought, to imagine stripping away all the layers she had built up over the years. To stand exposed in front of the world, raw and vulnerable. But for the first time, Amira realized that this was the only way forward. There could be no real healing without honesty.

Her phone sat on the table in front of her, its silence almost oppressive now. Amira picked it up, her fingers hovering over the screen as she thought about the decision she had made just days earlier to

disconnect from the virtual world. The quiet absence of it all felt both liberating and unnerving. She
couldn't remember the last time she had been so still, so present. There was no constant buzz, no social media updates dictating her every move. It was just… her.
still, the silence wasn't peaceful. It echoed in her mind, filled with questions. Why did I need to prove myself to others? Why did I think that being liked by strangers would somehow make me feel fulfilled?

Amira let out a deep breath, feeling the weight of the unanswered questions settle on her shoulders. But rather than running away from them, as she had done so many times before, she decided to face them headon.

She opened her notes app and started typing, writing out everything that came to her mind.

What do I really want?

I want to be more than just an image. I want to be seen, not as the girl who has it all together, but as a person—flawed, messy, and real. I want to find peace within myself, not from the praise of others. I want to stop being afraid of what people will think of me. I want to stop hiding behind the screen and finally live a life that's my own.

As she typed, the weight on her chest began to lighten. There was something therapeutic about putting her thoughts into words, about finally confronting her fears. She was tired of running. Tired of hiding. Tired of letting others define her. It was time to take back control, to stop being a prisoner of the digital world.

But even as she wrote, doubts crept in. Could she really change? Could she live without the constant need for validation?

The fear was still there, gnawing at her, but now, it was different. The fear wasn't as paralyzing as it once had been. She could feel herself slowly starting to let go of the grip that social media had on her, but it wasn't easy. Every day was a struggle. There were moments when she wanted to pick up her phone and check the latest updates, moments when the urge to go back to her old habits was almost unbearable. But she reminded herself that the only way out was through.

It wasn't just about deleting her social media accounts or stepping away from the online world. It was about reconnecting with herself. It was about rediscovering the things that made her happy before she got lost in the pursuit of perfection. She had to remember who she was before the likes and the followers had consumed her. She needed to find meaning outside of the digital world, to build real connections with the people who mattered.

The next day, Amira met with Maya at the park, their favorite place to hang out. Maya had been her best friend since childhood, and despite the distance that had grown between them over the years, Amira still trusted her more than anyone else.

As they sat on the grass, Maya looked at her with concern.

"Amira, you've been distant lately. What's going on?"

Amira hesitated, but then, with a deep breath, she decided to tell her the truth.

"I've been… lost, Maya," Amira said, her voice shaky. "I've been chasing after something that wasn't real. I thought that if I could just get enough likes, enough followers, I'd finally feel good about myself. But I don't. I feel empty."

Maya's eyes softened, and she reached out, squeezing Amira's hand. "I'm glad you're realizing this now. It's okay to feel lost. We all go through phases like that."

Amira smiled faintly. "I want to change. I want to stop living for other people and start living for me."

"That's a big step, Amira. But I believe in you," Maya said warmly.

Amira felt a surge of gratitude toward her friend. For
the first time in a long while, she didn't feel so alone. She realized that there were people in her life who loved her, who saw her for who she truly was, and that was enough.

Chapter 9:
The Path to Change

Change is often a word laced with fear, reluctance, and uncertainty. It is something we resist because it pulls us out of our comfort zones and forces us to confront the unknown. Amira knew this feeling all too well. She had spent her whole life building a digital persona, one that was loved and admired, but one that was also far removed from her true self. The idea of change, of stepping away from this carefully constructed life, seemed terrifying. Yet, deep inside, she knew that change was the key to finding herself again.

For Amira, the path to change was not a straight line. It was a jagged road filled with moments of doubt, frustration, and confusion. It felt like standing at the edge of a cliff, unsure whether to take the leap or stay safe on solid ground. But she also recognized that this was the path that would allow her to grow, to finally step away from the artificial world she had created online and embrace the life she was meant to live. Change was not something that would happen overnight, and Amira had to learn to accept that it was going to be a process—one that required patience, persistence, and courage.

The Fear of Change

Before Amira could even think about embracing change, she had to confront her greatest obstacle: fear. Fear had been her constant companion for so long. Fear of not being good enough, fear of losing her followers, fear of falling out of the spotlight. She feared what she couldn't control, what she couldn't predict, and what she couldn't hold onto forever. The fear of stepping away from the familiar comfort of her online persona was overwhelming, and the thought of being just another "ordinary" person without the validation of likes and comments made her feel anxious.

But Amira's journey toward change had already begun. She started to realize that the fear she was feeling wasn't a reflection of reality; it was merely a manifestation of her own insecurities. The world she had built online was only an illusion, a fleeting validation that didn't bring lasting fulfillment. She knew, deep down, that this wasn't the life she wanted to lead forever. But to take the first step, she needed to face that fear head-on.

The Decision to Change

The turning point came when Amira decided that enough was enough. She made the conscious choice to break free from the repetitive cycle of digital perfection and embrace the uncertainty of change. It wasn't an easy decision to make, but it was the most important one she had ever made. It was about taking responsibility for her life, her choices, and her happiness. It was about realizing that the likes and comments were not the true source of her value.

Amira had to let go of the past. The countless hours spent curating the perfect selfies, the desperate need for validation, and the constant comparison to others were no longer serving her. To move forward, she had to unlearn the beliefs that had held her back— beliefs that her worth was tied to her appearance and online popularity. Change wasn't just about deleting her social media apps; it was about changing the way she saw herself and her place in the world.

The Struggle and Resistance

Once Amira made the decision to change, the real struggle began. She felt the pull of her old habits— the need to check her phone every few minutes, the compulsion to refresh her feed, to see how many people had liked her photos. She was bombarded with resistance, that nagging voice in her head telling her that she wasn't enough, that she couldn't let go of the digital world.

Resistance took many forms: procrastination, selfdoubt, and even moments of guilt for stepping away from something that had given her so much attention. Her ego resisted, telling her that change was too risky, too uncertain. But Amira persisted, even when it felt like she was moving in circles. Every time she faced that resistance, she reminded herself why she had made the decision to change. She wasn't just running away from her past; she was running toward a new future.

Transformation Through Change

As Amira continued to navigate the path to change, she started to notice subtle shifts within herself. She was no longer obsessed with her phone or the approval of others. She began to prioritize her wellbeing, her mental health, and her relationships. Her thoughts were no longer consumed by what others thought of her; instead, she focused on what made her feel fulfilled and authentic.

Transformation, Amira realized, was not just about external changes. It was about the inner growth that allowed her to see herself as worthy without the need for constant validation. She became more aligned with her true self, more confident in her ability to create the life she desired. She recognized that the true source of happiness and fulfillment came from within, not from external sources.

The Ongoing Journey

Amira understood that change wasn't a destination; it was a lifelong journey. Even after she had made significant progress, there would always be new challenges to face. But she had learned that every step forward, no matter how small, was part of the process. The key was consistency and patience.

Chapter 10:
Facing the Mirror

Facing the Mirror

Facing the mirror is one of the most powerful acts we can do. It's not just about seeing our reflection; it's about confronting our true selves—our flaws, strengths, and everything in between. For Amira, it's a moment of reckoning. The mirror reflects not only who she is but who she has the potential to become.

The Fear of Facing Herself

Amira often avoids the mirror, afraid of the truths it reveals: mistakes she's made, dreams abandoned, and parts of herself she's neglected. It's easier to look away than to confront the emotions and insecurities hiding beneath the surface. But avoidance only keeps her stuck, disconnected from her true self. To grow, she must face herself with honesty and courage.

The Struggle of Self-Acceptance

Accepting herself, flaws and all, is one of Amira's greatest challenges. In a world that demands perfection, she often measures her worth by external standards. But true transformation begins with selfacceptance—acknowledging where she is without shame and embracing her imperfections as part of her unique journey.

The Importance of Self-Compassion

Self-compassion is essential for healing. Amira learns to treat herself with kindness and forgiveness, understanding that mistakes are part of being human. By letting go of harsh self-criticism, she creates space to grow and move forward with grace.

Embracing Her Shadows

Amira's shadow self—those parts of her she hides or rejects—holds valuable lessons. Facing her shadows allows her to integrate them into her identity and find peace. By embracing even the darkest parts of herself, she becomes whole.

The Power of Forgiveness

Forgiving herself is a liberating act. It's not about excusing her mistakes but releasing guilt and regret. By doing so, Amira frees herself from the chains of the past and creates space for a brighter future.

Conclusion: The Journey of Self-Discovery

Facing the mirror is about more than seeing what's on the surface—it's about discovering the truth of who we are. For Amira, it's a journey of self awareness, acceptance, and transformation. By looking inward with honesty and love, she unlocks the power to become her best self, one step at a time.

Chapter 11:
The Struggle Within

The Struggle Within

The human experience is marked by an internal battle we all must face—the struggle within. For Amira, this battle has been an ever-present reality. Behind her composed exterior lies a silent war of emotions, doubts, and dreams—a struggle often invisible to the outside world. Like many of us, Amira has learned to wear masks, smile through the pain, and soldier on, even when insecurity tugs at her.

The struggle within isn't a sign of weakness; it's what makes us human. It's about reconciliation— between who we are and who we aspire to be, between the mistakes of the past and the future we yearn for. For Amira, this tension has shaped her journey, urging her to rise above her fears and limitations to become the best version of herself.

The Battle Between the Mind and Heart

Amira often finds herself torn between her mind and her heart. Her mind, pragmatic and cautious, warns her to stay in her comfort zone, while her heart whispers of risks worth taking and passions worth pursuing. The clash leaves her in a familiar state of indecision: Should she play it safe or follow her intuition?

Amira has learned that this tension isn't about choosing one over the other but finding harmony.

She often reflects, "When my mind gives me structure, and my heart gives me purpose, I feel unstoppable." By letting her mind guide her with wisdom and her heart lead with passion, Amira strives to chart a path that's true to who she is.

The Voice of Self-Doubt

Amira often wrestles with self-doubt—the nagging voice that whispers, "You're not enough." It's a battle we all know too well. But Amira has learned to counter these thoughts by reminding herself of her worth. "I'm not perfect," she says, "but I've survived so much, and that in itself is proof of my strength." Self-doubt is not a reflection of our true potential. For Amira, managing it means practicing selfcompassion, silencing her inner critic, and celebrating her progress—no matter how small.

Perfection vs. Imperfection

As someone who once chased perfection, Amira has had to unlearn the idea that she needs to have it all together. "I thought being perfect would bring me happiness," she reflects, "but it only made me afraid to take risks." Now, Amira embraces imperfection as a part of life's beauty.

Instead of focusing on unattainable standards, she celebrates her journey, mistakes included. Her mantra: "Perfection isn't real, but progress is."

The Struggle for Control

Amira, like many of us, has a strong desire for control. She often plans meticulously, hoping to predict every outcome. But life has a way of throwing curveballs. Over time, Amira has learned that letting go doesn't mean giving up; it means trusting that things will unfold as they should.

"The more I resisted," she says, "the harder life felt. But when I surrendered to life's flow, I found peace." Amira's journey teaches us that true freedom lies in embracing uncertainty.

Action vs. Inertia

Amira often battles inertia. She dreams big but sometimes hesitates to take the first step, paralyzed by fear of failure. Her turning point came when she realized, "Even small steps count. Action creates momentum, and momentum builds confidence."

By focusing on progress over perfection, Amira has learned to overcome the pull of inaction. Her story is a reminder that the perfect moment to act rarely arrives—we create it through consistent effort.

Embracing the Struggle

Amira's story is not about triumph over struggle but learning to coexist with it. The internal battles—the tug-of-war between her desires, fears, and dreams— are what make her human. "I've stopped running from the struggle," she says. "It's part of who I am, and it's shaped me into someone I'm proud to be."

The struggle within is not something to fear. It's a catalyst for growth, a teacher of resilience, and a reminder that we are always evolving. Like Amira, we all have the strength to navigate our internal battles and emerge stronger, wiser, and more authentic on the other side.

Chapter 12:
Rebuilding Connections

In the intricate dance of life, relationships are the threads that tie us together. We are not solitary beings; we thrive through connection. Yet, throughout our journeys, we often face moments when those connections are strained, broken, or lost. Whether through misunderstandings, distance, betrayal, or mere drifting apart, the act of rebuilding connections is a profound and sometimes challenging process. Yet, it is a necessary step for growth, healing, and emotional fulfillment.

Rebuilding connections is not simply about fixing what's broken. It's about creating something new— re-establishing bonds that have been tested, reshaping the ways we relate to others, and rediscovering the importance of empathy, vulnerability, and trust. This chapter explores the complexities of mending relationships, the hurdles we must overcome, and the transformative power of reconnection.

Amira's Journey: Acknowledging the Break

For Amira, the first step in rebuilding any connection was
acknowledging that something had been broken.
It wasn't easy for her to admit that some relationships in her life had
drifted apart or been strained by misunderstandings. But Amira knew
that sweeping the hurt under the rug wouldn't heal the wounds. True
healing began with her courage to face the truth head-on and admit
that a connection had been fractured.

Whether it was with a loved one, a friend, or even herself, Amira
embraced honesty—both with herself and the people involved. She
realized that acknowledgment wasn't about blame or revisiting past
mistakes but about understanding that something important had been
lost and deserved to be restored.

Understanding the Cause

For Amira, the act of rebuilding could not happen without a deep
understanding of why things had faltered. Through introspection and
self-awareness, she started unraveling the reasons behind the
disconnection. Was it due to poor communication, unmet
expectations, or unresolved conflicts? Or perhaps life's inevitable
changes had pushed her relationships into the shadows?

Rather than pointing fingers, Amira chose empathy. She sought
clarity, both within herself and from others. By asking questions and

listening deeply, she began to understand the root of the problems. This

step helped her lay a foundation that wasn't about patching things up temporarily but about rebuilding something meaningful and enduring.

Vulnerability: The Key to Healing

Vulnerability had always been challenging for Amira. After experiencing pain and betrayal, it was natural for her to build walls. But Amira learned that healing required tearing down those walls and allowing herself to be seen—raw, imperfect, and real.

Her courage to share her thoughts, fears, and desires with the people she cared about created a ripple effect. It encouraged others to open up as well, fostering deeper and more meaningful bonds. Amira realized that vulnerability wasn't a sign of weakness but a bridge to true connection.

Trust: Rebuilding a Fragile Foundation

Trust was another hurdle for Amira. She knew that trust couldn't be rebuilt overnight, especially when it had been broken. Amira began to focus on actions rather than just words—showing up for her loved ones, being reliable, and staying honest even when it was difficult.

Through consistent effort, Amira slowly earned back trust and rebuilt it on a stronger foundation. It was a journey that required patience, but it proved to her that even the most fragile connections could be mended with time and care.

The New Beginning

For Amira, rebuilding connections wasn't about going back to the past but about creating a new, brighter future. Each relationship she rebuilt was stronger, more authentic, and rooted in deeper understanding.

Her journey of reconnection reminded her of the incredible capacity of the human heart—forgiveness, love, and growth. By facing challenges with grace and determination, Amira proved that broken bonds could lead to new beginnings, richer and more meaningful than ever before.

In this process, Amira didn't just rebuild her relationships—she rebuilt herself. And in doing so, she discovered the true beauty of connection: a journey of shared vulnerability, growth, and love.

Chapter 13: Finding Balance

Amira had always been a person of extremes—her emotions, her goals, her relationships. At times, she gave everything of herself to others, to her work, and to her passions. At other moments, she withdrew completely, retreating into the safety of solitude to avoid the noise and chaos of the outside world. For a long time, Amira lived in this cycle, not knowing how to find equilibrium between her inner desires and the outer expectations placed on her. It was only through her journey of self-reflection and rebuilding connections that she began to understand the importance of finding balance.

The Push and Pull of Life

In the past, Amira often found herself overwhelmed, caught in a constant tug-of-war between the demands of her family, friends, and career. She felt like she had to be everything to everyone, and whenever she failed to meet one of those expectations, it left her feeling like she was falling short. She gave so much of herself to the people she loved, to the point where she had little left to give to herself.

Her work, too, had been an area of imbalance. Amira had always been driven, ambitious, and eager to prove herself, but her work had consumed her. Long hours, late nights, and endless meetings left little room for her to enjoy the simple pleasures of life. And even when she was physically present, her mind was often still tied to work—an endless loop of thoughts that prevented her from truly being present in any moment.

As she sat in her favorite quiet corner of the café, reflecting on all that had changed, Amira began to realize that true peace would not come from doing more or being more. It would come from understanding that life was not meant to be lived in extremes, but in balance. The balance between work and rest, between giving to others and giving to herself, between being driven and allowing space for joy.

Prioritizing Self-Care

One of the first steps toward finding balance was acknowledging that self-care was not selfish—it was essential. For years, Amira had neglected her own needs, putting others before herself. She thought that by taking care of everyone around her, she would somehow feel fulfilled. But she learned the hard way that it was impossible to pour from an empty cup.

As she embarked on her journey of healing, Amira began to recognize the importance of nurturing her own well-being. This didn't mean she had to abandon her responsibilities or stop caring for others; it simply meant that she needed to create space for herself. Whether it was a few quiet moments with a book, a walk in the park, or taking a day off to rest, Amira understood that these moments were not luxuries—they were necessities for maintaining balance.

Slowly, she began to carve out time in her schedule for self-care. She started to listen to her body, to recognize when she was fatigued, and to honor those moments by taking a step back. For Amira, finding balance meant that she was no longer apologizing for needing time for herself. It meant setting boundaries and respecting her own limits, which, in turn, allowed her to be more present and engaged when she was with others.

Balancing Relationships

Another area where Amira struggled with balance was in her relationships. She had always been the kind of person who gave wholeheartedly, believing that the more she gave, the closer she would become to the people she loved. But she came to realize that true intimacy didn't come from overextending herself—it came from quality, not quantity.

During her conversations with Amina, Nadia, and Sara, Amira learned the importance of setting

boundaries in relationships. She couldn't be everything to everyone, and trying to do so only led to burnout and resentment. She needed to find a balance between being supportive and allowing others to support her in return. Her relationships needed to be reciprocal, with both giving and receiving in harmony.

Amira also recognized that balance in relationships wasn't just about time or energy—it was about emotional equilibrium. She learned to communicate her needs honestly and to allow her loved ones to do the same. Gone were the days of assuming everything would be fine without addressing the underlying issues. In her pursuit of balance, Amira embraced vulnerability, sharing her fears, joys, and challenges with those closest to her.

The Dance of Balance

Finding balance was not a destination—it was a continuous journey. Amira realized that there would be times when her work would require extra attention, and other times when she would need to focus on her personal life. The key was flexibility. Balance was not a rigid equation, but a fluid dance that adapted to the rhythm of her life.

Sometimes, Amira would feel out of balance, pulled in too many directions, and it was important for her to acknowledge that feeling without judgment. She learned not to expect perfection from herself or her life. She understood that some days would be more challenging than others, but as long as she kept returning to the principle of balance—where both her inner peace and outer obligations were in harmony— she would find her way.

Amira's journey toward balance was not easy, but it was transformative. By letting go of perfection, embracing self-care, and setting boundaries, she created a life that was aligned with her values and needs. The extremes no longer dictated her life. Instead, she learned to embrace the ebb and flow, knowing that with each wave of life, there was an opportunity to recalibrate and restore balance.

Chapter 14: A New Beginning

The sun was setting on the horizon, casting a golden hue over the city. Amira stood at her window, gazing out at the world below. It had been a long, winding journey to this point—one that had been filled with struggle, growth, and transformation. But as she looked at the fading light, she realized that the moment had finally arrived. A new beginning was waiting for her, and it was time to embrace it fully.

For so long, Amira had been trapped in the past, carrying the weight of old mistakes, missed opportunities, and unspoken regrets. She had allowed these shadows to define her, to limit her potential. But now, standing on the threshold of a new chapter in her life, she felt a sense of release. It was as if the weight had lifted, and she was free to move forward.

The path ahead was uncertain, filled with both promise and challenges. But for the first time in a long while, Amira felt ready. Ready to let go of the stories that no longer served her. Ready to write new chapters, not defined by the past but by the person she had become.

Embracing Change

Change had always been a difficult concept for Amira. She had resisted it for as long as she could, fearing that it would disrupt the life she had known. But over time, she had come to understand that change was not something to fear—it was an inevitable part of growth. Every experience, every lesson, and every setback had prepared her for this moment.

Amira's journey had been full of difficult decisions, but she had learned to trust herself. She had shed the layers of doubt and fear that once held her back. She no longer felt bound by the expectations of others or by the limiting beliefs that had once shaped her life. This new beginning was hers to claim, and she was determined to walk forward with courage.

She remembered the countless nights spent overthinking, unsure of what the future would hold. But now, those worries seemed distant, like echoes of a past version of herself. Amira had come to realize that the only constant in life was change itself. The key to navigating it was not to resist it, but to embrace it. With that realization, she felt a sense of peace settle over her.

The End of a Chapter

In many ways, this new beginning was the end of an era. It was the end of the Amira who had been lost in self-doubt and insecurity. The person who had been afraid to take risks, to make bold decisions, and to step into the unknown. But it was also the end of the person who had clung to old relationships, old routines, and old habits, afraid to outgrow them.

As Amira reflected on the relationships that had come and gone, she realized that some people were meant to be in her life for a season, and others for a lifetime. Some bonds had been broken beyond repair, but that didn't mean they were failures. It simply meant that they had served their purpose. Amira had learned from each of them, and those lessons would stay with her forever.

It was also the end of the constant striving for perfection. Amira had spent so many years trying to meet impossible standards, both for herself and for others. But now, she understood that perfection was not the goal—growth was. She had learned to be kind to herself, to accept her flaws and embrace her imperfections. She was no longer chasing an idealized version of herself; she was learning to love the person she had become.

The Courage to Begin Again

A new beginning required courage, and Amira knew that it was not always easy to take that first step. There were still moments of fear, moments when the uncertainty of the future seemed overwhelming. But Amira had learned that courage was not the absence of fear—it was the willingness to move forward despite it.

She thought about the dreams she had once put on hold, the aspirations that had been buried under the weight of everyday life. It was time to breathe life into them again. Whether it was starting her own business, traveling to new places, or exploring new creative pursuits, Amira knew that this was her chance to build the life she had always imagined.

The future was no longer a distant dream—it was now. And with that realization, she felt a renewed sense of purpose. She didn't have all the answers, and she didn't know exactly what the future would look like. But she was no longer afraid to pursue it.
She had learned to trust the journey and trust herself.

Letting Go of the Past

For Amira, the new beginning was also about letting go. Letting go of the past that had held her back. Letting go of the pain, the regrets, and the anger that had been weighing on her heart. She had spent too long carrying these burdens, afraid that if she let go, she would lose something important. But now, she understood that the only thing she had been losing was peace.

Amira had learned that forgiveness, both of herself and others, was the key to moving forward. She had spent years holding on to grudges, unable to release the hurt that had been caused. But in doing so, she had only trapped herself in the past. Now, she was ready to release those chains. She was ready to forgive and to free herself from the heavy emotions that had held her back.

As Amira let go of the past, she felt a lightness in her heart. It was as though a weight had been lifted, and she was finally free to move forward without the burden of what had once been. She no longer needed to carry the mistakes of the past with her; she could leave them behind and step into the future with an open heart.

Moving Forward with Hope

Amira's new beginning was not without its challenges. There would still be obstacles, setbacks, and moments of doubt. But she knew that she had the strength to face them. She had come so far, and she had built a foundation of resilience that would carry her through whatever came next.

The road ahead was still unknown, but Amira felt a sense of excitement, not fear. She knew that every new day was an opportunity to create something meaningful, to make a difference in her own life and in the lives of others. She was no longer defined by her past mistakes or the limitations she once believed in. She was free to explore, to grow, and to build the life she had always dreamed of.

Amira took a deep breath, looking out at the world once more. The sunset had given way to the soft glow of the stars. A new beginning was here, and she was ready to embrace it.

With courage, with hope, and with the lessons of her past guiding her, Amira stepped forward into the unknown, knowing that whatever lay ahead, she would face it with strength and grace.

Chapter 15: Embracing the Journey

The road that lay before Amira was long and winding, but for the first time in a long while, she felt at peace with its unpredictability. She stood at the crossroads of her life, no longer seeking perfection but welcoming the challenges and flow of the journey. The lessons she had learned, the struggles she had overcome, and the person she had become all led her to this moment. There was a quiet beauty in the uncertainty, and she understood that every step—no matter how difficult or unexpected— was part of a grander narrative that was unfolding just for her.

Amira had spent so many years resisting change, wishing she could control every outcome and predict every turn. She had thought that to live fully, she needed to have all the answers, all the plans neatly laid out. But now, she realized that true fulfillment didn't come from knowing what would happen next. It came from surrendering to the flow of life, from letting go of the need to control and simply embracing each day as it came.

The Dance of Life

Life, she had learned, wasn't a destination—it was a journey. It was a series of moments, each one interconnected with the next, like a delicate dance. Sometimes, the rhythm would be slow and gentle, while other times it would quicken, pulling her in unexpected directions. There were moments when she stumbled, when the music seemed to fade, and she would wonder if she had lost her way. But always, the beat would return, steady and unbroken, inviting her to join once more.

For so long, Amira had resisted this dance. She had feared stepping out of sync, afraid of being caught in a misstep. But now, she understood that every misstep was a lesson, every fall a chance to rise again. It wasn't about perfecting the dance; it was about being willing to move, to sway, to step forward with courage, even when the music felt uncertain.

She thought about the times when she had resisted change, when she had fought against the natural flow of her life. She had tried to force things to fit, to make sense of the chaos around her. But now, she realized that life wasn't meant to be controlled. It was meant to be experienced. It was meant to be felt. **Finding Beauty in the Unexpected**

Amira had learned that the beauty of life lay in its unpredictability. The unexpected twists and turns, the moments of serendipity, the people who entered her life when she least expected it—these were the things that made the journey so rich and meaningful. Had she not embraced the unknown, she would have missed out on the extraordinary moments that had shaped her into the person she was today.

She thought about how far she had come—from the person who once feared uncertainty, to the woman who was now willing to dance with it. The journey had taken her through dark valleys, but it had also led her to breathtaking peaks. It had shown her that even the most difficult moments had beauty in them, even if it was hard to see at first. Each challenge, each setback, had offered a lesson, a gift wrapped in the form of struggle. And now, she could look back and see how each piece fit together, creating the beautiful mosaic of her life.

Amira realized that she was no longer waiting for life to become something she could control. She was living it fully, in all its messy, unpredictable glory. The joy was in the journey itself, not in reaching a specific destination. She understood that life's true purpose was not about achieving perfection or success; it was about living authentically, embracing every moment, and trusting that each step, no matter how small, was leading her exactly where she needed to go.

The Power of Acceptance

One of the greatest gifts that Amira had given herself was the power of acceptance. She had learned to accept both the beauty and the pain of her journey. In the past, she had been so focused on what she thought should happen that she failed to appreciate what was. But now, she saw the richness in every experience. The joy, the heartache, the growth—it was all part of the process. None of it was wasted. All of it had shaped her into the person she was becoming.

Acceptance didn't mean resignation. It didn't mean giving up on her dreams or settling for less. It meant embracing life as it was, with all its imperfections, and understanding that sometimes the most beautiful things emerged from the most challenging moments. Amira had learned that the key to peace was not in resisting what was, but in accepting it fully.

This sense of acceptance was freeing. It allowed her to let go of the constant need for validation, for approval, for perfection.

It allowed her to stand in her truth, to trust herself even when things didn't go according to plan. She no longer needed to justify her path or explain herself to anyone. The journey was hers to take, and she was ready to embrace every twist and turn with grace.

The Strength of Patience

Amira had also learned the strength of patience. In a world that often demanded instant results, she had come to appreciate the quiet power of waiting, of letting things unfold in their own time. She understood now that some things couldn't be rushed.
Growth, healing, transformation—they all took time.

There had been moments when Amira had been frustrated with her progress, when she felt like she
wasn't moving fast enough, wasn't achieving enough. But now, she recognized that the greatest transformations happened in the spaces between action. The times when she allowed herself to rest, reflect, and simply be—those were the moments when the most profound growth occurred.

Patience was not about sitting idly by, waiting for things to change. It was about trusting that everything was unfolding as it should, even when she

couldn't see the full picture. It was about showing up, day after day, putting in the work, and allowing the results to come in their own time. Amira knew that life wasn't a race, and there was no need to rush. She was exactly where she needed to be.

Walking with Gratitude

As Amira continued her journey, she felt an overwhelming sense of gratitude. Gratitude for the lessons learned, for the people who had touched her life, for the opportunities that had come her way. She had come to understand that gratitude was not just about being thankful for the good things—it was about embracing all of life, with its ups and downs, with an open heart.

Gratitude had transformed the way she viewed the world. It had shifted her focus from what was lacking to what was abundant. It had allowed her to appreciate the simple moments—the warm sun on her face, the laughter of friends, the quiet stillness of the early morning. These were the moments that made the journey worthwhile.

Trusting the Journey

Above all, Amira had learned to trust the journey. She understood that there would be times when the path seemed unclear, when the fog of uncertainty would cloud her vision. But she also knew that this was part of the process. The journey would not always be linear. There would be detours, roadblocks, and unexpected obstacles. But that was okay. She was no longer afraid of the unknown. She trusted that each step she took was leading her closer to her true self, even if she couldn't always see where it would take her.

In the quiet moments, Amira could hear the whisper of her soul, urging her forward, reminding her that she was exactly where she needed to be. Every experience, every choice, every lesson—had led her here. And as she embraced the journey, she knew that there was no destination to reach. The journey itself was the gift.

As Amira stood at the crossroads of her life, she realized that trusting the journey didn't just mean going with the flow—it meant fully embracing the uncertainties that lay ahead. She had spent so much time trying to control every detail, wanting to know exactly what would happen next, and feeling frustrated when things didn't go according to plan. But now, she could see the wisdom in the ebb and flow of life, the way things unfolded in their own time, without her having to force them into being.

There was a peace that came with trusting the journey. It was the kind of peace that came from knowing that she didn't have to have all the answers right away. The next step would appear when it needed to, and she didn't have to rush to figure everything out. Life would unfold in its own rhythm, and all she had to do was show up, do the work, and be open to the possibilities.

This realization brought a sense of freedom. Amira no longer felt burdened by the pressure to have everything perfectly planned. She didn't need to know exactly where she was headed because, in the grand scheme of things, it wasn't about the destination—it was about the path, the experiences, and the lessons learned along the way.

Moving Beyond Fear

Trusting the journey also meant moving beyond the fear that had once held her back. Fear had been a constant companion throughout her life, whispering doubts into her ear, telling her that she wasn't good enough, that she wasn't worthy of her dreams. It had kept her stuck in old patterns, afraid to take risks, afraid to step outside her comfort zone.

But now, Amira understood that fear didn't have to control her. Fear was just a natural response to the unknown, to stepping into new territory. It was not a sign that she wasn't capable—it was a sign that she was on the verge of growth. She realized that every time she pushed through her fear, she discovered a new part of herself, a new layer of strength she never knew existed.

Amira had spent so many years allowing fear to dictate her decisions. But now, she was learning to step forward despite the fear, to take risks and trust that she had the strength to handle whatever came her way. It wasn't about eliminating fear—it was about moving forward in spite of it, knowing that the rewards would be worth the discomfort.

Final Reflection

Amira's journey had been nothing short of transformative. She had come a long way from the girl who had once been paralyzed by doubt and fear, unsure of her place in the world. The girl who had spent her days chasing after perfection, convinced that happiness and success were things to be earned, not discovered. But now, standing on the threshold of a new phase in her life, Amira realized that her true transformation had come not from achieving anything externally, but from discovering her own inner strength.

The themes of her journey were woven throughout her experiences: trust, growth, vulnerability, and the courage to embrace uncertainty. The path had not always been smooth, but it had always been meaningful. Each hardship, each moment of fear or discomfort, had taught her something new about herself. And with each lesson, she had grown stronger and more confident in her ability to face whatever challenges came her way.

The final realization for Amira was that the journey never truly ends. It isn't about reaching a destination, but about continuing to evolve, to grow, and to trust the process. Life is a constant flow of changes, opportunities, and challenges. The key is not to resist them, but to trust that each moment is part of the larger picture, even when we don't fully understand it.

About the Author

"I am Maryam Husain, a corporate professional by day, but a writer by heart. With years of experience navigating the world of business, I have developed a deep understanding of people, their quirks, and what makes them tick. I have learned that life is often best understood through a mix of logic and a little bit of humor.

A girl with a passion for storytelling, I use my experiences to create characters and narratives that are both relatable and thought-provoking.

I currently live in Delhi, balancing my professional life and writing aspirations, while continuing to observe the human experience with both laughter and a deep understanding…

A Tribute to Amira

Amira, once lost in fear and doubt,
Fought through storms to find her route.

Each fall was deep, each step was slow,
Yet through the pain, she learned to grow.

The mirror once showed a face unsure, Now it reflects a soul
so pure.

Amira's tale, a beacon of light,
From shadows to strength, she shines so bright.
For those who feel lost, her story shows, The courage it takes
to let hope grow....